FIRESONG: A LETTER

by

Amy Leigh McCorkle

Copyright December 2025

For Laurel Adler and Jeremy Allen White, Laurel for her support, Jeremy for his inspiration

Chapter 1

Cash Black stood on the penthouse balcony questioning what had led him to this night this place.

The winter breeze in Louisville hit his bare chest and chapped his fingers gripping the railing.

Groupies lay passed out all over his room.

His jeans fit but even though it was freezing he was in his socked feet. The sounds of Desert Rose danced on the air.

He held a bottle of beer his twelfth or thirteenth and draining it.

He'd gotten the news earlier that most of his band, including his girlfriend Rosa had gone done over the Ohio the day before.

He climbed to the wall and held his arms out.

It would be so easy to let.

But then like a twisted fairytale the sound of glass shattering wrenched his from suicide plans.

A woman flew down screaming.

Her hand made contact with his railing. Reflexively he reached for her and caught the other hand.

Quickly he jumped down and shouted, "Climb!"

As they both fought for her life, their eyes met her desperation met his grief. A surge of energy went through him and he pulled her all the way back up by her waist. They landed, him on his back, her on her stomach facing him.

Neither could talk, both breathless.

He became aware.

Her eyes were blacked. Her lip was busted. Head was bloodied.

"No ambulance."

"What do you mean?"

"He'll kill me."

There was a pounding on the door.

They sat up. He placed a finger to her lips.

Cash stood up and shut the balcony doors and curtains. Then answered the door. A tall brute of a man towered over him.

"Can I help you," Cash played up the drunk lothario people saw him as.

"I'm sorry I was looking for my girlfriend."

"No problem. Good night."

Cash shut the door. He headed towards the balcony and brought her inside.

Took her to the bathroom.

He held her hands and said, "We've both had a rough night."

She said nothing.

He began cleaning her wounds. Led them to the shower and lowered them to a sitting position. He turned the water on and she leaned into his embrace and she comforted him as his quiet tears fell.

IT HAD BEEN TWO WEEKS since the plane crash and murder attempt on the stranger. It had shook him to the core. His next album had been delayed until he put another group together. And the woman. He didn't get her name. But for the night they had been the answer to each other's pain.

No sex.

Just the kind of emotional intimacy that comes along once maybe twice in a lifetime.

The plane crash and the woman. They dominated his evert thought.

He was an artist. A poet. A rocker.

But the crowds had been getting smaller and smaller. His sales dwindling. Capitol Records said he was going to have to do a greatest hits album or worse, a Christmas one.

When he asked about a third option they presented something which made him want to vomit.

Bring in a female artist, an up and coming one for him to collaborate with.

"Are you fucking crazy?" he asked. "I just lost my entire band."

His producer, Marc, hadn't been on the plane. He had survived. Maybe he could make the executive Donna see reason.

Donna leaned forward, "This woman has real song writing chops. Give her a full chance. She was given her choice of artists to work with. She chose you specifically."

"Well isn't that special.'"

Donna picked up her phone. "Send Hope in. You behave."

It was like waiting forever.

Finally the door began to open.

It was two weeks ago.

He was at the penthouse.

Hope entered. The mystery woman from that night and he came face to face.

"This is Hope Rosen."

"Finally a name to put to the face."

He took her hand and it was magic.

"I will leave you two to it."

Donna escorted them out.

"Cash Black, don't mess this up."

"Lunch?" he asked her.

"Sounds perfect."

Chapter 2

They sat across from one another, devouring the Diner's specialty of the day, pot roast and potatoes.

"Hard to believe you'd like a place like this," he said with a wink and a nod.

"Why? This stuff sticks to your ribs. Besides other places would charge twice as much for the same food and it wouldn't taste as good."

"Hope you're an interesting cat."

"You mean because I have nine lives."

"The way you fell out of the sky you'd think I carried a multitude of 4 leaf clovers in my pocket."

"That's an odd way of putting it."

He took the bread and sopped up the sauce. "If you hadn't interrupted me I would have jumped."

She slowly set her fork down, and cleared her throat. "If we're confessing things, I'm living out of my car. And this is the first thing of substance I've eaten since the room service you ordered that night."

Cash froze mid-bite.

"Why didn't you come find me?"

"We didn't exchange names. Besides, you Cash, freaking, Black and I'm a no name domestic violence victim."

"If that night is any indication of what you've been through you are not a no name."

"That night was epic. In such a disastrous way."

"Everything happened so fast. I haven't been able to stop thinking about you."

"Me and my cat Nancy's car is parked a couple of blocks from here."

"It's freezing out there."

"She's bundled up and she's a registered service animal, so when I go into coffee shops to work she sits in her cat stroller I write and play my guitar."

"Sounds romantic."

"Until you realize the reality. I'm on the run from my brute of an ex Bruce, and if he got a hold of us he'd torture and kill us."

"Capitol in Nashville has some sleeping quarters and a shower. I could talk to them on yours and Nancy's behalf."

"Is it really a good idea?"

"I think it's the best thing for all concerned."

"I have no savings to speak of. I'm down to my last bit of cat food. I'm sure I'll be eating trash soon enough."

Cash leaned forward and touched her hand.

"Come stay with me. My mansion is huge, I have a guest room and an in house studio. We can work there and when we're ready to do your album we can move to the Capitol Records studio. More than that, you and Nancy will be safe."

Hope tapped her coffee spoon to the table.

She leveled him with a strong gaze.

"Okay. Let's go."

Cash held his hand up and called out, "Check please."

HOPE ACROSS THE THRESHOLD with Nancy in her bubble backpack. Hope stared in wonder as they moved through the mansion.

Cash looked to the white and orange tabby.

"I don't think Nancy knows what to make of this place," Cash chuckled.

"Or her owner," Hope responded.

Cash laughed softly. They came to a stop in front of a small room. "Listen, I have some arrangements to make. Make yourself at home. If you get borrowed or lonely Sam will be by in a few hours."

Hope slipped out of her backpack. She proceeded to set it down on the bed and said, "Say thank you to the nice man Nancy."

"No need, just get to writing."

"I thought we would be working together."

"And we will. I just need to run some errands first."

He walked out of the room and Hope freed Nancy from her carrier. She sank down on onto the bed and cradled Nancy to her chest.

She gently pet Nancy,

"We're not in Kansas anymore Nancy."

CASH WALKED THROUGH the house.

He crossed paths with the head of his security detail, Sam.

"Another one?"

"No, this one's different. Keep her safe. Especially from a guy named Bruce."

"Yes Sir."

The limo pulled up and Cash stepped in. As he pulled off he awaited the demo at Capitol.

Chapter 3

Cash sat in Mark's studio, the two of them passing a blunt. "Cash, you took her home. You took her and her cat home. Do you really think that's wise."

Cash inhaled, waited a long minute then exhaled.

"We saved each other's lives. What was I supposed to do. She walked in and when we had lunch I learned her cat and she were living in a car. In the dead of winter."

Mark leaned forward. "I know you just lost Rose. But diving into another relationship isn't the answer."

"I put her in a guest room. I left her in the care of Sam. I did not sleep with her."

"But you're thinking about her."

Cash sighed and admitted, "I haven't stopped thinking about the events of that night or the connection we had."

"And now that you know she can sing and write, at least in theory, it's even more intense."

"I guess. That night I was so low and drunk and she was so scared and vulnerable...I bound us together."

"Do you hear yourself talking? You've never talked about anyone this way. Not even Rose."

"Don't remind me."

"Why not, you need to be reminded. The music industry can eat the strongest souls alive. And she ain't it."

Cash killed the blunt and stood up. He said, "On the contrary Mark I think she's stronger than any of us."

Mark rolled his eyes. Cash served him the middle finger and left. He needed to vet Hope's musical skills. Before signing on completely.

HOPE SAT IN THE WINDOW seat with Nancy in her arms playing Amy Lee and Seether on the radio, singing at the top of her lungs.

She'd been by herself all day composing lyrics and scripting melodies.

She kept coming back to the moment Bruce had tossed her through the balcony window and by some miracle she'd grasped the railing and Cash Black had come swooping into her life.

That night had been a mix of magic and horror.

The horror of Bruce and the magic of the emotional intimacy that she and Cash had shared in one another's arms.

Now she just wanted to sing.

Pages of notes and lyrics were scattered around beneath her. She continued to sing to her cat.

She was lost in her thoughts, totally unaware of Sam guarding her, or of Cash walking up. Cash said nothing as she belted out the end of the under appreciated Bond Theme, Another Way to Die.

Cash clapped vigorously.

"Bravo," he said.

Hope screamed at the top of lungs. "You scared the shit out of me."

"Well, at least we know you've got the pipes to sing. And I can see you've been writing, now to see if you're as great a writer as you are a singer."

He went to stoop down. Hope let Nancy down who jumped up on the bed. Hope shoved Cash out of the way and started scooping, grabbing and snatching lyrics up and from Cash's hungry hands.

"What the..."

Hope became emotional. "These are unfinished private experiences."

"We're supposed to be working together, don't you trust me?"

"Yes. No. I don't know."

She crumpled the sheets up and fell to the floor. Shutting down.

"Neither of should be alive. The night connects us."

She looked up at him with such openness and vulnerability he joined her on the floor. "What if Bruce finds me?"

"I'll kill him before I let him finish what he tried to start."

"I'm so sorry about your band, and your fiancée."

"Girlfriend. Premature death is how rumors get started. I loved her. I'll grieve her. But we were on the downside of our relationship. My band, on the other side I'll never be over."

"I saved Nancy. Waited for Bruce to leave the house. Took the basics and my car and left Louisville in the review."

"Family?"

"That was the hardest part. I'll endanger them if I contact them."

"You love them."

"Very much."

"I'm sorry Bruce is stalking you."

"Maybe he'll get bored."

"Let's hope."

"Hey you made a funny."

They chuckled. He took her hand and their foreheads touched.

Cash swore to himself he would keep her safe and reunite her one day with her parents.

Chapter 4

They stood outside of the record label. Mark watched them, he understood what Cash was feeling. He'd saved her. But there was something else. She had seen him through that night too. This could be magic. If she could sing, If she could write. There were many pretenders to the throne. But no one could equal Cash. Seeing them talking, deep in conversation maybe, just maybe, this could be this generation's Johnny and June.

"Let's take a selfie, put some good juju out there for us," Cash said.

"Sounds great!"

Cash tossed him the phone and the fast friends began to pose and make silly faces. When Cash did something unexpected he whisked her into his arms and twirled her around in a circle. She blushed and he sat her to her feet.

Mark snapped so many photos Hope was cracking up and Cash was treating her with such preciousness he could feel the sparks coming off of them.

"Okay, time for work."

They walked in dancing to Sexyback towards the studio.

Mark felt their joy. Their excitement. Their anticipation. The nervousness.

He was watching the most unexpected love story play out in front of his eyes. It was catching. But he was grieving Rose, hard. They had been sneaking around Cash's back. While Cash was no angel the affair still carried the weight of true guilt.

Seeing his friend start to move on so quickly also engendered feelings of envy.

They arrived in the studio.

There were a few electric guitars, an acoustic, an amp, and a synthesizer. Microphones and buffers.

"Toto we're not in Kansas anymore," Hope said looking around in wonderment.

Mark took a seat behind the glass.

The plan was to let Hope take the lead. But Cash followed her into the studio proper. He shut the door and took her hands in his.

He looked deep into her eyes, and said. "You can do this."

She closed her eyes and took a deep breath.

"What song do you want to test and develop first."

"Crushed."

"Okay, let's roll."

She stood in front of the microphone and cleared her throat. She picked up the acoustic guitar.

She quickly tuned it. She started to strumming a melody and Cash placed the headphones on her.

"Give bass and snare."

Mark was impressed. She knew her shit.

She opened her mouth and proceeded to break hearts and draw an audience.

"I am on the outside looking in/the glass cracking/the blood leaving out of me/free falling through the sky/your hand catches mine/we both should have died that night/ instead your hearts pain healed mine."

Tears started to fall. Not for Hope but for Cash. His heart cracked open as she sang the final verse.

"I would have been trapped in a world of fists/and broken bones/your touch forgave me/your touch smoothed the pain away/I looked in your bluest of blue eyes and/falling I continued/falling forever into you."

Hope stepped away from the microphone and set her guitar aside.

Cash walked up to her wiped her tears away.

"That was beautiful."

Mark pressed the speaker. "That's what we call a one take wonder."

Hope looked at him and something broke open inside of her and she fell sobbing into his arms.

It didn't matter they had an audience.

It didn't matter they were both crying.

The pain of their mutual loss spoke to something much deeper.

"That was the work of a poet," he whispered.

"I don't know if I can go on."

"You can,"

"You don't understand."

"Try me."

"I have bipolar disorder."

"So."

"I've been without my medication for six weeks. I can't adult. I can't life."

"We'll get you your medication. We'll get you what you need."

Cash held Hope's face and kissed her with a tender, lingering kiss and then again.

"I promise you," he said, "it will all be okay."

He lifted her up and walked passed the gasping crowd that had gathered. Including Donna who turned to Mark and said, "This could be very, very good or very very bad."

Chapter 5

Hope stood back and watched Cash as he grieved at the crypt. His hands were in his blue jean pockets.

Cash flashed on what their last moments must have been like.

Smoke in the cabin.

People screaming.

The woman crying and saying their last words and texting their last messages. He'd yet to open those messages. The guilt weighed too heavily on him.

He reached out and touched the marble.

Hope walked up to him and touched his arm.

He jumped. "It's not your fault you know that don't you?" Hope said.

"Maybe. I hear their screams. I feel them crying. I can smell the smoke." Cash's voice cracked.

"Not. Your. Fault."

"That's easy to say for you."

"Come here."

She hugged him and held him.

He found himself clinging to her and her warmth.

Tears fell down his face and he found himself pulling back and caressing her hair and her face. He was mesmerized by her beauty. He could tell she was having a hard time meeting his gaze.

"What are you afraid of?"

"That this fear and my sickness will dominate the rest of my life."

He held her by her arms.

"You're not alone. And man can you tear a heart out with words."

A single tear dripped down her face.

He wiped it away.

Gently touched her lips with his. Noting they had healed nice that night in the penthouse. He let the kiss linger.

Her mouth parted and a tender fire erupted warming them both. Their hands moved the flame seemed to burn brighter than anything he'd experienced.

The emotions wrapped them up tighter.

They continued to kiss, and make out.

The freezing cold pushed them closer to one another. Their lips parted and Cash pushed Hope against the wall of the crypt.

Their breathing was labored.

He ran his hands up and down her arms.

They kissed again. This time the tenderness gave way to passion.

He nuzzled her neck. She sighed. And when they kissed one another one more time it was an inferno that neither could get enough of.

"Is this a good idea?" Hope asked.

"It feels right to me."

"What if your fans don't like me?"

He trailed kisses down her neck. Then gazed at her. He touched her tenderly again. "I don't care."

"I care."

"Why?"

"I don't want to be seen as the gold digger. Homewrecker."

"How do you feel now? What are you thinking now?"

"I'm on fire."

He pinned her hands above her head.

His mouth was on hers in a cataclysmic rush. His tongue gently prodding her mouth open and entering her world, and hers his.

Cash grabbed her legs and wrapped them around his waist.

They grinded core to core.

Hope threw her head back. Nothing had ever felt so good. She had never trusted a man so much. She hang onto him and began whispering to Cash.

"Yes Cash, yes Cash. Now. Now."

She began to weep and he pushed harder and harder.

He looked into her eyes.

Those emerald green eyes.

They were falling for him. And he was falling for her.

"Yes angel."

"Say it Cash," she murmured.

"I love you, angel."

"Call me by my name."

"I love you, Hope."

She cried out in pleasure and he captured her mouth in a kiss. She loved him. God help her she loved him too.

Chapter 6

Cash watched Hope sleep with Nancy curled up on top of her in his studio while he nursed a glass of scotch.

It was snowing much like it had been that night the plane crashed. The he and Hope can hurtling into each other's lives.

He'd yet to give a statement.

How could he. He'd been a terrible boyfriend. And now that she was gone, he knew Hope was right, she would have to prove herself separately from him.

Because if she didn't the world might hate her.

How could they. She had a voice that could set hearts aflame, and soothe the beast in any man.

There she was with her companion keeping her guard.

He poured another glass of his finest malt scotch, Sam knocked on the door.

Cash sipped his drink and waved Sam in.

"Have you seen the news?" Sam asked.

Cash placed a finger to his lips.

Sam walked over to the television and turned it on.

The news anchor read the copy while the video to their secret meeting of how they met and saved one another's lives.

Seeing himself standing on the ledge. Hearing her scream.

"Turn it off."

"Why didn't you tell me?"

"I said turn it off."

Hope stirred. Sam turned the television off. For a moment all was silent.

"I knew there was something going on I just didn't know what it was."

"No wonder you are shielding her."

"You can't tell anyone who she is."

"This is everywhere. As soon as her boyfriend comes looking what do you expect me to do?"

"I expect you to protect her anonymity. And her life. Exactly like you do with me."

"Are you sure you want that?"

Cash looked at her and back to Sam, "I love her Sammy."

"You love a lot Cash."

"No, Sammy, I'm in love with her. And I will do anything for her to live a life she's dreamed of."

"People will see her as a gold digger."

"Watch you mouth," Cash hissed.

"How do you propose to prevent."

"I'll come up with something."

"That's not a plan."

"When her songs are ready she'll tour with me."

"Do you think that will work?"

"I don't know really, all I know is it will buy me some time. More importantly it will buy Hope and Nancy some time."

"Okay. Your word is my command."

"Thanks Sammy. Now if you don't mind, if I could have a moment with Hope."

The security guard walked out of the office and shut the door.

Cash could hear the screams. All of them. Then finally they faded and only one remained. Hope's.

Grief flooded him.

For his bandmates. Even Rose. But he was transfixed by Hope and the ginger and white tabby.

He had to tell her they were all over the news. People would be able figure out who he was. And because she was an ordinary citizen for now they would track her down soon enough. Bruce was a danger to them all.

It was only a matter of time until he would become a problem.

But Cash laid down next to her and rested his hand on Nancy.

"They're after me, aren't they."

"They're after us," Cash corrected her.

"It was Bruce."

"You're safe."

"My Dad is a cop, he taught me to use a gun a long time ago."

"There's too many guns in this world as it is."

"I will protect me and you and my baby," Hope said.

"I will protect you, Nancy and all that you love."

"I'm so sick of the violence."

"Peace. I bring you and Nancy peace."

Chapter 7

Bruce stood in his apartment smoking a Marlboro Red and drinking a Guiness. A gun hanging in his hand.

The television prattled on about his ex. They didn't know it. But he did.

He thought she had killed herself.

She had lost her mind that was the only reason he had thrown her out the window. He had grieved her and their cat Nancy.

Now to realize they were alive, most likely under that musician's care, he puffed the cigarette and exhaled.

He stood up and aimed his gun at the television.

Bruce hesitated. He towered over the set laboring to breathe.

""Fucking bitch. I'll kill you both."

Standing 6'5 and hulking with muscles he took a step back and brought the hammer down.

Once. Twice. Three times.

STRANGELY ENOUGH, NO one noticed them.

Hope and Cash walked hand in hand, ball caps on, oversized sunglasses shielding their faces, into the studio.

"You think the world knows who those two strangers on the balcony were?" Hope asked.

"I hope not."

"Did you see the news last night?" Donna said sweeping into the recording booth.

"Yes," Cash said removing his sunglasses.

Hope took off her hat and glasses.

"By the way you are behaving I imagine you both have."

"Save it Donna."

"Considering you were about to take a header off the balcony Cash, you should be grateful Hope's mystery man threw her out the window."

Cash pinned Donna to the wall and roared.

She looked genuinely terrified.

"You will protect Hope. You hear me. Any harm comes to her I will find you and spill the tea on all your major clients."

Hope placed a gentle hand on his shoulder.

"Easy, Cash. Don't be what Bruce was to me."

Cash stepped back. "Sorry Donna. I'm going through some things."

"Obviously. Listen to your new friend."

"Donna. I'm ready to cut an EP with several songs. Let Cash take the lead."

"You're album is a duet with four to five solos each with three songs featuring one another. You about your heartbreak and Cash about the loss of his childhood band."

Cash was not thrilled.

He did not like to be told how to create. Especially in such a personal way/

"No. Creation doesn't work that way."

"I don't think you have a choice."

"What are you talking about?"

"Your sales are down. You have an album due. And it's either this one or a Christmas album. As for Hope, and her safety we'll assign an extra detail to her. You all need to be focused on the album."

Donna started to walk out and Cash put his fist through the drywall.

Hope pulled him into her embrace.

"We'll figure it out."

Cash broke down in sobs. He clung to her in such a way that a child would a parent.

She kept talking.

"I won't let anyone get to you."

He kissed her passionately and kicked the recording booth door shut.

He smoothed her hair back.

"I don't deserve you," he said, tears in those brilliant blue eyes of his.

"I never expected this."

"Hold on for the ride of your life."

HOPE STOOD UP CLOSE to the microphone and sang a few verses.

Mark said, "Give me it to me again."

Cash looked to Mark. "What are you talking about that was perfect."

"You forget. I'm the producer,"

"You've never been this involved."

"Yes I have."

"Not in a while."

Mark looked away. He did not want to have this conversation now.

"What was that?"

"Cash, let's not do this."

"Mark you have produced me for years and for the last few it's been different. What aren't you telling me?"

Mark turned to the recording booth. "Hey Hope, take five. Grab some water."

"Everything okay."

"Yeah, me and Cash need to have a coming to Jesus talk."

"You sure Cash," she asked.

"I'm good. Be safe."

She left them alone.

Suddenly the tone of the room changed.

"I know."

Mark swallowed hard.

"I wasn't who I was supposed to be for Rose, but I will be for Hope. I know you two were having an affair. If you can forgive me for not loving her, I can forgive you for doing so."

Mark and he embraced. Pounded each other's back.

Hope returned.

Mark smiled. Cash said, "Let's cut the record."

Chapter 8

Hope and Cash sat at the diner where they first ate enjoying a shared plate of hot cakes and steak and eggs.

Hope was practically glowing.

"This had been the most wonderful day of my life," she enthused. She took a bite of egg.

He took a bite of biscuits and gravy. "Damn this is good."

"Comfort food is the best on rainy days."

"And on successful days."

"Cutting three songs in one day," Hope said.

"I'd say so," they both laughed.

Suddenly Hope's smile vanished.

"Is it something I said," Cash said, then turned towards the door. "Shit."

Bruce sauntered to their table.

"So this is where you skipped off to," Bruce said.

"I'm lucky I skipped off anywhere thanks to you."

Cash cleared his voice. Bruce kept staring at Hope with that dark menace Cash remembered from that night a month ago.

"If you don't mind this is a date. A private conversation. Kindly see your way out of it."

Bruce snickered. "He's funny. You like that now Hope? I thought you liked brute force."

"I like knowing I won't be beat up for me being myself."

Cash stood up. He nodded at Sam.

"Bruce, you like intimidating people so much allow me to introduce you to my bodyguard. His name is Sam."

Sam joined them at the table.

"Anything wrong Cash?"

Cash smiled and said, "No. Bruce was just leaving. Weren't you?"

Bruce smiled, his teeth yellow. "This isn't over."

Sam positioned himself between the couple and Bruce.

"You heard the man. You don't leave now, I'll escort you out. And I don't mean there will be sweet nothings at the end of the evening either."

Bruce held his hands up and started walking backwards. "Message received. But Hope you can't be guarded all the time."

He turned around and walked out the door.

Cash reached out and touched her hand. She sat frozen, silent tears falling.

"Will I ever be free?" she asked.

Cash squeezed her hand. "Yes."

"I can't eat."

"We'll get it to go."

Sam held up his hand, "Check please."

CASH DROVE THE WINDING road to the new observatory.

"Where are we going?" Hope asked.

"My favorite place to go when the world is just to much to deal with."

"How is it I've never been to this part of town?"

"My guess Hope, you were trying to stay invisible."

"I was. Places like these are peaceful but going alone can leave you open to attack and with no hope of survival."

"You are stronger than you know."

Cash pulled to a stop just a few feet from the observatory.

Hope took her seatbelt off and said, "When I'm writing I feel so free. When I'm singing and performing I feel like I'm letting people in the only way I can. And when we well, when we were together at the crypt I felt we were grieving together in a different way."

Cash took off his seatbelt and turned to her.

"You are an incredible singer/songwriter. I didn't think we would work together. But that was before I saw you walk through the door."

"Here's the thing, I've never been on a live stage before."

"So."

"So?"

"Small audiences. Solo in my bedroom. Personal stories are my thing. I didn't plan on falling for a superstar. And I certainly didn't count on him being my superhero."

"You are superstar in the making. You will break free."

"Really. I believe sometimes and then I will be eating my meal and minding my own business and the boogie man will pop up from my past. How do I grab peace from the chaos."

Tears fell down her face.

Cash reached out and wiped them away.

"You are going to soar higher than you ever have. You hear me."

He could hear his own voice crack.

They embraced.

Holding onto one another close and not letting go.

Chapter 9

Hope was in her room sleeping curled up with her kitty Nancy. He was locked away in his studio, angry rain pelting the roof. Listening to the unfinished tracks of his and the band's unfinished last album.

He'd been busy helping comforting Hope.

Now he was the one who needed help.

He leaned back with a guitar on his chest tapping it along with it.

How did he feel?

Bereft. Morose. At a loss. As if a butter knife was carving into his heart.

Suddenly Big Mike's voice boomed. "I know you're heading home for the holidays, but I wanted to say we've all been worried about you. You're channeling brilliance. But it's angry and dark. Some of us might be making this the last tour with you. Not me, but some others don't like this turn. So, get some rest, get some help and we'll bang out this record after Christmas."

His gaze focused on the Bullitt bourbon and glass then to the vision of Rose standing in his doorway.

"Why are you throwing me away?"

"I'm not."

He poured more Bullitt. He drank it.

"You've already slept with her. At my grave."

"That had nothing to do with you."

"It had everything to do with me!" she shouted.

"Rose, we weren't in love anymore."

"You cheated on me regularly. I loved you."

"I'm broken Rose."

"Then what's with this new girl. What makes her different?"

"She wasn't sleeping with my engineer."

Rose's apparition sat next to him. "That's bullshit. You know what I think it is?"

"Pray tell."

"She's touched something in you. When she was headed to her death and you were headed that way too, something changed within you and chose life. That was an intense connection. And whatever happens you'll always share that night. I doubt anyone will be able to penetrate that."

"What am I suppose to do with Bruce?"

"I don't have all the answers. I would recommend calling the cops. Upping security. And dial back on that stuff in the meantime."

She stood up and as she walked away she faded into nothingness.

"Rose, don't go."

She heard her voice one last time, "The way forward is through."

He picked up the bottle and pressed repeat on the demo.

Sitting back down he chugged the bourbon and blacked out.

HOPE STIRRED. SHE OPENED her eyes to Nancy kneading her stomach. That was followed by a roar of pain. Nancy leapt off the bed and scrambled under the bed.

Hope gingerly stepped out of bed.

She peaked out the into the hallway.

She heard another cry of pain. It was Cash. He was sobbing.

Each cry cut deep into her soul. She rushed through each room in the mansion until she found Cash in the bathroom laying on his back in the walk in shower. With a straight razor in his hand.

He sobbed.

Hope knelt down next to him, "No, no, no. Hang on. Just let go of the razor."

She slowly moved to take it and he pulled it away, nearly slicing her open.

His eyes widened as they met Hope's compassionate ones. He dropped the razor. Hope pushed it out of the way.

She laid down beside him as he shivered and shuddered and hiccupped.

She could smell the booze on his breath and coming through his pores. She just didn't know if this was a regular occurrence or one triggered by grief and guilt.

He rolled into her arms.

"Are you cold?"

"I'm numb."

"I know the feeling," Hope acknowledged.

"We're you numb that day at the crypt?"

"No. It was the first time I'd felt something in years other than pain."

"Bruce is a real threat."

"If you hadn't helped the night he threw me out of the window above yours we wouldn't be having this conversation."

"If he hadn't I'd be dead too."

The shower rained down on them both.

He touched her face, and said, "You were my salvation that night."

"Your eyes, I see music in them. I feel your heartbeat in them."

"You're not a songwriter. You're a poet like me."

Cash and Hope kissed and their mutual pain came together and faded. No longer two, but one.

Chapter 10

Cash was in the booth now, desperately trying to find the opening musical phrase to first of the last tracks.

Hope was on the other side of the glass noodling around the chords in her head. She knew Cash was not looking for help.

Here, in the now, he was looking to the past. He was looking for guidance from ghosts and the guilt of the ending of a relationship he did not treat with respect.

He was lost. Looking to collaborate but afraid to at the same time.

She longed to connect to him they way they had been. She spun her pencil around and tapped her eraser on her notepad.

"So sick about it. We said goodbye before I was ready. What goes up must come down and you slipped through my fingers. Why did you walk away? Why did you make me cry…" she hummed and as if on cue Cash began the track they had laid down before the holidays.

"Like a merry-go-round we go up-up-up and down-down-down. We had love, but was true. Was it lasting. Was it meant to bleed. Or was it meant to die…"

Mark stared at Hope then turned on the speaker. "Cash I think Hope should be in there with you on this. She might have the answers to why this isn't coming together for you on this."

"No offense Mark you're an engineer and producer not an artist."

"I give up." Mark threw up his hands and started to walk out of the studio.

Hope touched his arm, "Let me try."

She took a breath and steeled herself. With two brave steps she entered the lion's den. Hope was smart enough to know when in the presence of danger and right then all signs were screaming at her to run screaming and find her cat.

Her legs felt like spaghetti. Her knees were threatening to buckle. Her chest was tight. But in a short time, she had grown to love him. Maybe not to die for him level but to live for him and embark on a creative journey definitely.

She began to shut door when Mark called.

"No, don't—," Mark called trying to stop her.

Hope proceeded to pick up her guitar and sit down at Cash's feet.

Then placed the tuning bar on it and strumming and picking and humming.

Cash met her gaze, the savage beast meeting the beautiful muse of music.

"Amazing grace, how sweet the sound, that saved a retch like me. I once was lost but now am found."

"'Twas grace that taught..."

Tears dripped down his face as he sat down and the two of them played old gospel and hymnal songs."

Mark quietly stepped to the board and flipped the record stripped back the acoustics, sat down and listened.

What he heard was soothing, beautiful, and soulful.

Two kids from the south harkening back to a seemingly simpler time.

Though he knew Cash's past. And he was privy to those painful lyrics and suicidal and homicidal images that would inextricably link them together if not musically, then in the public eye forever.

This was a side he had never seen in fifteen years. Watching them fall deeper in love over music was something he knew was special.

Even though he was angry at Cash for failing Rose. He would fight to protect what he was watching bloom before his eyes.

HOPE WAS SLEEPING IN the recording booth while Cash and Mark sat and listened to what Mark had recorded.

"They're not looking for a coming to Jesus album," Mark said. "But good Lord does your pain, and longing, and loss come through."

"It's the emotional honesty that I've been searching for on the last album."

"You never struck me as a man of faith."

"When I was kid, Mom would take me to Saint Christopher's Cathedral. My father would work eighty hours a week then spend his Saturday night's drinking. When he got I would hear them fight. Then those footsteps. He would beat the shit out of me. Later on we found out Dad suffered from bipolar disorder. It can run through my veins like a poison. Since the plan crash I've been avoiding treatment."

"You can't be doing that now. Especially with a woman to protect from a monster."

"And an album to tour and promote after it breathes for a minute."

"You don't mean..."

"The five duets are the five songs Hope walked me off the ledge with. The solos are next. Shelve the three duets we cut yesterday and start from scratch."

"A faith album."

"An album about finding peace and love."

"You never struck me as a romantic."

"There's a first time for everything."

Chapter 11

Cash sat in his therapist's office. Quietly waiting for his arrival. He twisted and pulled at his sleeves wishing Doc Lawrence would hurry up.

The previous days had been a mix of nightmares and daydreams.

He preferred to think about the daydreams, like Hope's voice soothing the savage beast inside of him.

Not of the nightmare Bruce crashing their delightful breakfast. And not the worries it engendered of Hope being alone.

Doc Lawrence walked through the door in his tweed jacket and bowtie. He grabbed his notepad and pen and sat down across from him. Cash could feel the energy vibrating from his stomach to his chest to his fingertips.

Therapy was not something he had chosen initially. It had been forced upon him. But recent events had pushed him to reaccess.

The death of his band.

The premature loss of a girlfriend.

The introduction of a woman and musical partner. It was all too much. At least to handle on his.

Even though his faith was as strong as ever, it was obvious it would take more than just Jesus. It would take therapy. It might even take medication.

"Cash, I'm here for whatever you need. Start where you want. End where you need. Or don't. Just know this is a safe space."

Cash took a breath. He closed his eyes and he was six years old in a storm cellar while the storm raged within and without.

His parents said nothing.

Suddenly he was back in the office.

"When I was a kid I was afraid of storms."

Doc Lawrence looked at him and asked, "Why?"

"Aren't all kids scared of storms?" Cash asked.

"Some, but there must be a reason you're mind went there first."

"When I was very young a tornado ripped through the town in the middle of the night. Mom didn't survive. Dad never got over it. So whenever I heard those sirens I thought, that's it, the gods are going to take me or take dad now. I would start to cry. Dad would be fine. Then when the storm passed he would get drunk and take a big ass paddle to me. It was then I began praying God would take one of us so we could break the cycle."

"You're still here."

"So is Dad," Cash said pointing to his head. "He visits every night. And because of that I have no peace."

"And you're afraid of getting close to a woman because of that."

Cash grew quiet and started cracking his knuckles. Standing up, he walked to the door. "I'm sorry Doc. I can't do this. I thought I could do this but I can't."

Cash swept out the door.

He kept replaying his mother's death over and over.

Tears started falling.

"I won't fail you, Hope. I promise."

Cash walked into Capitol Records and took a deep breath. He promised. He would not fail her.

HOPE SAT IN THE RECORDING booth shivering.

She wanted to go somewhere and be alone. Well maybe not completely alone. She loved being in the recording booth and listening to Cash perform.

She also loved performing. And listening to her songs come to life.

But after last night she wasn't sure she had what took.

She needed to get into a psychiatrist's office as well as a therapist's room.

She could feel the threads on her sanity beginning to loosen.

Many people had claimed to be her north star over the years. All of them had been full of shit.

Her trust in God was what it was. She had to be careful that she differentiated between her faith and the symptom of religious ideation. One was a tool in her healing, the other was her sickness.

In all the Churches she had sought out only one had made her feel welcome and not inherently damaged.

Messiah Trinity.

When she took off to the streets of Nashville she left it and it's comforting embrace behind.

She sat in the window seat of the guest room looking at pictures of her mom and dad. She wanted so badly to reach out and touch them.

But she couldn't.

Not yet. But one day. And soon.

Chapter 12

Cash walked into his home, only to be greeted by Nancy winding her way around his ankles. She purred and meowed at him lovingly. He stooped down and stroked her fur.

He stood back up.

He stepped forward a few steps, his boots clicking against the hardwood floors. Then stopped.

In the stillness he heard water in the kitchen running.

His heart began to hammer against his chest.

He started walking towards the sounds.

Then stopped and picked up Nancy and placed her safely away in the bathroom downstairs, He pulled out a switchblade.

The hair stood up on the back of his neck.

"Hope!"

She didn't answer.

His voice rose in urgency. "Hope are you okay."

He rounded the corner and found her sprawled out on the floor. Cash tenderly rolled her over. Savagely beaten. With multiple gunshot wounds.

Cash had told Sam not to leave her alone.

"Nancy," Hope murmured. "My baby."

"Nancy's okay."

Cash dug out his phone and dialed 911.

He grabbed her hand.

"Dispatch 911 what's your emergency?"

"Break-in at 2345 Brooklawn. A woman has been shot. Her name is Hope Grenwell."

"Who am I speaking to?"

"Cash. Cash Blue."

"Ambulance and police on the way. Stay on the phone."

"You hear her Hope. Stay with me. Stay with me."

CASH WALKED INTO THE emergency room, with Sam and Mark on his heels. A few steps behind them was Donna purse on her wrist, phone in her hand.

"I want the press release to read new up and comer shot by abusive ex protecting her baby cat Nancy. Cash rushes her to the hospital. Uh-Huh. Full stop."

Cash's head was about to explode.

"I'm here with Hope Grenwell."

"She's in surgery. Have a seat."

"I am the one who found her. I am responsible for her. I am fucking Cash Blue and you are going to take me to her or get me more than she's in surgery."

Mark reached for his arm.

Cash shook with rage, tears of impending grief ran down his face.

"Sir, I know you're upset. We're doing the best we can."

Cash labored to breathe and headed straight the vending machine grabbed it by both sides and roared. He swung hard and it took Mark and Sam holding onto him to prevent him from destroying it and his hand.

He collapsed into them.

"You didn't see her. Man you didn't see her."

"I stepped out to get her dinner. I was gone twenty minutes tops," Sam said brokenly.

Cash grabbed him by his collar and seethed, "I told you not to leave her alone."

"I know, I'm sorry."

"Did you not get it? Did you not see her fall out the window? Did you not see her the morning after?"

"Yes."

"We're just getting through the loss of the band. Mark is just getting through the loss of Rose. You get that? You get that!"

"Mr. Blue," the surgeon's voice cut through the rage and fear and grief.

"Where is she?"

"She's still in surgery. She's made it through the initial stages of danger. She's stable now. There's really nothing you can do."

"Don't tell me to go home," Cash said through clenched teeth.

"Mr. Blue."

"Don't fucking tell me to go home."

Mark placed his hand on Cash's shoulder.

"Nancy," he said.

Cash said, "Bring her here."

"You're crazy."

Cash insisted, "Hope needs to know Nancy is okay. She's in the downstairs bathroom, Feed her, water her, and bring her here."

Mark looked to Sam and said, "We got your back dude."

Sam headed out the door.

Mark led him to the couch. Donna brought him a water. They looked at one another. If Hope died it would be catastrophic.

Donna set her phone down and said, "It's going to be okay."

Cash murmured, "You didn't see her. You just didn't see her."

He leaned back and started holding on to his cross around his neck.

Chapter 13

Cash slept in the chair wrapped in a blanket, Nancy purred in her backpack. Hope stirred.

Nancy popped up and meowed. "Nancy?" Hope murmured.

Cash opened his eyes.

"She's right here. She's okay."

Tears slipped down her cheeks and she said, "Can I see her? I need to see her."

Cash tossed the blanket back and gingerly scooped Nancy out of the bag. He walked over to Hope and laid her cat on her chest.

She cried, cradling her and stroking her fur.

Nancy sniffed her and licking her tears away.

"Baby you're really okay."

"She is," Cash said.

She looked at him. "What about you?"

"I'm fine."

"Where's Bruce?"

"There's a manhunt right now underway."

Nancy curled up between them and Cash laid down next to her.

"You should runaway from me."

"Never," Cash said.

"You're too noble for your own good."

Cash half laughed half cried.

"Me, noble?"

"Imperfection doesn't mean toxic."

"How would you describe Bruce?" Cash asked.

" A monster," Hope seethed as tears dripped down her face.

"I would agree."

"What if the record label drops me because of this?"

Cash took a deep breath.

"Donna is spinning this in our favor, you'll at least get the first album out. After that it will depend on the sales of the album."

"So the pressure is on."

"That's a way of looking at it."

She pet Nancy.

"There are situations where it is easy to create. The music just takes you places that only one other person understands. At least in the creation process. And when you set it free it suddenly bursts onto the scene and it's not just yours. It's complete."

Cash smiled down at her and said, "I've never head it so beautifully put."

"Looking into your blue eyes the words come easily."

"When I look into your brown ones it's easy to conjure feelings of true love and the magic of forever."

He touched her face.

"You and I, we have a real chance at making it don't we."

"Is that a question or a statement?"

"Maybe a bit of both."

He tenderly took her in his arms and said, "We do, don't we."

The cat meowed.

Hope laughed and for the first time joy split her heart open in two and she felt like there could indeed be a future.

CASH WALKED IN WITH Hope and Nancy to the house.

It was the first time in a month that his house didn't feel like a crime scene. He looked to Hope, she held Nancy in her backpack close to her chest.

Hope on the other hand was back for the first time since that night in question.

"We can go someplace else."

"Cash I can't keep running. We have an album to finish. Then we have to go on tour. I may need professional help but I will not let him win."

Cash put his arm around her.

"I've heightened security measures. Security gates. Private security detail."

"Sam?"

"He's feeling pretty guilty. He feels like he could have prevented it."

"That's ridiculous. Bruce is a nasty piece of work."

"He is."

They took a look at the house.

Hope stared at the kitchen.

"I'll be glad he's in prison."

"I will be too, Hope. I will be too. Let's go upstairs to the studio."

Chapter 14

Hope sat across from her therapist.

"You've been through a lot. And now you're going to be facing recovery while working. That's a stressful."

"Bruce still hasn't been captured. There's that."

"How are you holding up?"

"How do you think? Other than that Mrs. Lincoln."

"Sarcasm."

"It's a defense mechanism."

"There's no need for combative dialogue. This is a safe space."

"People say that all the time."

"This is though. Emotionally. And with your private detail outside keeping watch with Cash you should feel more relaxed than you have."

"The man who tried to kill me twice is still roaming the streets. Pray tell, how am I supposed to relax?"

"It's normal to be scared given your circumstances. But Hope, you can't live in that place and move forward. You're embarking on a relationship, a new and healthy one. You have a music career that's blossoming. You're no longer living out of your car."

"And I'm grateful for all of those things. Bruce haunts me though."

"How serious are you and Cash."

"We made love, once. Now we communicate through music."

"Is there any intimacy."

"Emotional intimacy yes. Creative connection. There's nothing like it."

"I meant have you had sex."

"No, not since the burial at the crypt."

Her eyebrows raised.

"We weren't naked and nobody saw us."

The therapist held her hand up. "No judgement."

"Dawn, you have to be kidding me."

"I'm not. We all do things we regret."

"I don't regret being with him."

"Hope…"

"We've saved each other, why would I leave him?"

"Have you thought about being on your own, exploring your independence."

"I was homeless for a month with my cat Nancy, why would I want to go back to that?"

"Hope, you are a capable artist and person,"

"That I know."

"You don't need a man to succeed."

"No I don't but when Cash and I perform together, I don't care what you think, when you hear it, you'll feel the magic we do."

Dawn set her pen down and smiled.

"I don't think I've ever seen you like this."

"Like what?"

"In love."

Hope leaned back in her chair. Sometimes little realizations like that were what carried her through.

CASH STOOD IN THE STUDIO playing back a demo of Hope's.

Her voice like crystal washing and cutting through him.

Her voice shouting and piercing through the noise in his head.

The pain touching his soul.

All from a simple demo.

Even he couldn't do that at her age.

She was 28 years old. He was 35 going on twelve. But where she was concerned he would do anything for her. Live for her, die for her, kill that bastard Bruce for her.

A new song started, the raw authenticity that was coming through took his break away.

It took him to the night where Nancy greeted him at the door and led him to Hope.

Lying on the ground.

Shot, beaten, and left for dead.

She had one thing on her mind Nancy.

That demo would make the record.

That record would become one of his bestseller and would put her on the map.

Hope had already marked his heart.

It was time to go public.

Bruce be damned.

Sam came in and said, "She's home."

"Bring the car around."

"You sure boss?"

"I'm positive."

Chapter 15

"Where are we going?"

Cash turned the radio up and together they cranked out All I Really Want by Alanis.

"You didn't answer my question," Hope said.

"Somewhere special," he replied.

"I thought you already had."

Cash laughed.

"I got some news while you were in the therapist's office."

"What kind of news," Hope asked.

"The kind you and I have been waiting for."

"Is it about the record?"

"No. Law enforcement has apprehended Bruce."

"Get out of here," Hope said leaning forward.

"Not kidding. You can really start to heal without having to worry about him."

"I think I'll always have to worry about him in a way but I'd be saying I wasn't relieved in a way."

"Have you thought about want you want to do now that he's behind bars."

"I'm afraid to trust it. I'm afraid to trust me."

Cash reached out and took her hand.

"Hope, there's nothing you can't do."

"Swear?"

"I do."

"Where are you taking me?"

"Just wait."

Halloween was a thing to Hope. As was Thanksgiving and Christmas. Even in the darkness they all meant something to her.

Candy. Food. Presents. The music. Holiday traditions. The movies and cartoons. The romance and family celebrations.

The holidays gave her hope ironically enough.

And simple pleasures like long car rides with Cash seemed to be coming back in a rush.

The battles in her head seemed to quieting down.

Song after song came on and note after note they sang.

They eventually came to a stop at Gus's Famous Fried Chicken. There was a single car parked and waiting for them.

"What is this?" Hope asked.

Sam pulled up alongside them and got out.

"No press," Cash said rolling his window down.

"No press," Sam repeated.

"Everything set up."

"Absolutely."

Sam gave two thumbs up and Cash said, "Help Hope. I'm going to head inside."

Cash stepped out and trotted inside.

Sam walked around and opened the passenger side and helped Hope out. As they neared the entrance Cash came back and intercepted them.

Cash held her arms and kissed her on the cheek.

"I worked hard to arrange this. I waited for the right time. For when you would be up to it."

"Up for what?"

Cash held out his arm and Hope gingerly took it.

Sam held open the door.

Hope couldn't process what was going on at first. Balloons. A banner. And her family. Her mother June, her father Jon and her sister from another mister Dawn.

She lost her breath and stood stone still.

Tears easily fell.

"Mom, Dad...Dawn?

She turned to Cash.

"How? Why?"

"Because you deserve all the things."

Her family ran to her and took her in a group hug. All of them hugging and crying.

"We've missed you," her mom said.

"I've missed all of you."

"We were he had harmed you."

"Dad..."

"Oh baby," he said touching her cheek.

Dawn cleared her throat. "Don't ever disappear on me again."

"Oh you..."

They embraced tightly.

Sam and Cash smiled. For the first time in his life Cash knew he had done good.

Chapter 16

Hope walked through the house with a bottle of champagne and two champagne flutes. She was barefoot and in her Golden Girls pajamas. And looking for Cash.

Usually he was in the recording studio.

But tonight he was AWOL.

Instead she heard him pacing above head. She went up the foyer steps and went from room to room until she got to his bedroom.

It took a moment to realize he wasn't pacing. He was pounding on his guitar. She knocked lightly on the door.

"Everything okay in here?"

Cash hurled his guitar across the room.

Hope's eyes widened.

The remorse registered in his face.

Hope froze.

Cash stammered. "I-I don't know what came over me."

Time seemed to slow down, she took a deep breath and set the glasses and champagne aside.

"I won't do this again."

Cash walked into Hope's embrace.

"I'm sorry."

"I know."

"I won't do this again."

Hope wanted to walk away. Another abusive and volatile man was not something she wanted nor needed. She knew Cash was a good man and was the anti-thesis of Bruce.

"Why are you spiraling?"

Cash was drowning in images of a plane going down. Flames. His band screaming. And Hope lying on the floor and her blood on his hands.

He buried his face in her hair, pain cutting deep.

A single hard sob erupted from his chest.

"Forgive me."

"I forgive you. But we have to get therapy."

"Together."

"Of course."

He pulled back and held her face.

Catching her tears as they fell.

"Tonight was so beautiful."

"Yes it was," Cash replied.

"It's been so long since I've seen them all. Seeing Dawn was especially wonderful."

"I know Gus personally and his chicken is the best."

"It was so warm and intimate. A piece of me thought I'd never see them again."

"I wanted your reunion to be perfect."

"It was."

"How about some of that champagne?"

"Sounds good…"

Cash lifted her off her feet and twirled her around then set her to her feet.

Cash kissed her impulsively and Hope lost herself to him. Wholey. Utterly. Completely.

CASH LAY ON TOP OF Hope. Gazing into her eyes. Making love to her in a way he had not allowed himself to any woman, including Rose. Maybe especially Rose.

The way Hope moved and sighed and looked at him. They were one. In his arms, in his bed, it felt so right.

It were as if they had been searching for each other all their lives and had finally found one another.

Hope, for the first time and felt profoundly at ease.

She felt like she could trust Cash.

That she could trust him to not be another Bruce.

The way he moved inside of her was ecstasy.

They kissed as the moment reached togetherness and Cash rolled to his side.

Holding each other there was an intimacy they both knew they had longed for in someone else that they were finding in each other.

"What's this?" Cash asked, touching the cameo like picture on her necklace.

"That was Chyna. Nancy's predecessor."

"What happened to her?"

"What happens to all animals, she crossed the rainbow bridge."

"Bruce didn't...?"

"Chyna came before Bruce. Sometimes I think Bruce would hurt Nancy to hurt me. And that scares me."

"I won't let him, Hope."

"I believe it."

They curled into one another's embrace and each of them drifted of to sleep.

Chapter 17

Hope woke up and rummaged around for her notebook.
"There we go."
She next to a sleeping Cash scribbling a song she had been trying desperately trying to birth since that night they had met.
The lyrics flowed smooth and easy.
She could even hear the melody.
She looked back at the words and tears came to her eyes, Chills ran up and down her arms.
She got up out of bed and grabbed Cash's guitar and picked up her slip of paper with the song written on it.
Hope started playing and quietly singing.
Cash stirred. She didn't seem to notice. He sat up. Chills going up and down his body.
There was a haunted sound to her voice. But rocked at the same time.
Even as she sang he could hear his own voice running underneath parallel in a soothing seductive way.
Suddenly he was humming along and they having that magical symbiotic creative moment.
He had never experienced something like this.
He reached out for his shorts and pulled them on. Walking over to her he stood across from her and they completed the song.
"That's the magic baby. You're really going places."
"We're going to go places."
"I've gone places.."
"We're going to go places and we're going to help a lot of people."

"From your lips to God's ear."

Hope set the guitar aside and stepped into Cash's arms and they began to dance.

DAMON KNOCKED AT THE door. A plain clothes detective he popped a tums.

This case was getting to him. Really getting to him.

He usually carried his emotions buried beneath a six pack of beer and a 3 pack a day habit.

But when he laid eyes on that video he supposed he was just as transfixed as anyone else. No he was standing at the rocker's house shielding the woman from Bruce Backer and the rest of the world.

Damon had yet to question either about the night in question. The focus had been on capturing Bruce, monster that he was he eluded capture for far too long.

He had a rap sheet a mile long.

And this mystery woman, Hope, had somehow survived a massive attack.

Now he needed to question them.

He knocked again.

The security officer Sam Hernandez answered the door.

"Oh you."

Damon sighed, "Are they available?"

Sam stepped back and allowed him entrance, That was better than most responses they were getting. But whatever. Damon just wanted to build a solid case against the bastard who had spent the last few months terrorizing this woman.

Hope and Cash were already waiting for him in the living room.

Cash stood up and shook his hand.

"Thanks for accommodating us by coming here. Please take a seat."

Damon sat down and said, "It's not a problem. I think we all want the same thing."

"We do," Hope admitted.

"Well, you both will be happy to know, Bruce is being help without bond until trial. As well as being a flight risk, his attacks on you make him a considerable to you and society."

"That's actually good to know," Hope continued.

"Now, I know this will be difficult but if you can walk me through what happened during the second attack..."

Hope instinctively reached out for Cash. Cash reached back.

"I had just finished giving Nancy a bath. I heard the door and called out for Sam, thinking he had returned with the carryout. Then-," she took a breath and continued. "Then I turned around and saw Bruce. I screamed. He pulled out a gun and then nothing."

"Nothing?" Damon asked.

"Everything is a blank."

"Oh. Have you spoken to a therapist?"

"Is it bad that I haven't?"

"No, Hope, you've done nothing wrong. But it would help you remember and in turn help the investigation."

Cash said, "You don't have to do anything you're not ready for."

"No, I want to help. I want Bruce out of commission."

"As do we all." Damon smiled kindly.

Hope shook. Cash embraced her. Damon stood.

"That'll be all for now." He handed Cash his card. "If you need anything let me know."

"Thank you Detective. Sam, if you'd see him out."

Damon could tell this had brought the couple closer. He wanted to give them all the chances at the making it. So he would do his best to put Bruce behind bars permanently.

Chapter 18

Hope sat in the window seat, sipping Earl Grey and staring out the window as it snowed.

Wrapped in a blanket she listened to the songs she and Cash had already cut in the low fi way. Talking to the detective had been arduous. It had taken a lot out of her and she just wanted to be alone.

Nancy sauntered into the guest room and leapt up on her lap.

Hope scratched her behind her ears and stroked. "I know pretty girl it's been a long day."

Nancy walked up her chest and licked her face. Catching the few tears she had left to fall.

There was a knock at her door.

"I really don't think I can handle another peptalk."

"I don't have one for you," Cash said leaning against the door frame. "I thought you might like this though."

He held a book in his hand and walked towards her.

She swung her legs around and Nancy jumped down.

Cash sat down next to Hope and handed her the book.

Hope opened it. The cover was worn and the pages were yellow and dog eared. She looked the title page. It read Cat's Cradle by Kurt Vonnegut. First Edition.

Tears filled her eyes.

"How'd you know he was my favorite author?"

"Call it an educated guess."

"It's my favorite book by Vonnegut."

"You're a brilliant writer."

"I think there's some question to how you figured this out."

"Well I asked Dawn what comforts you and she said Daniel Craig movies and Kurt Vonnegut books."

"She knows me well."

""I've invited them all for dinner tonight. Is that alright."

"God yes. I've missed them terribly and Thanksgiving is coming up. I was thinking we could decorate the house the day after Thanksgiving. Make a pot of chili and make a day of it with everyone. Mom, Dad, Dawn, Sam, even Mark."

"Hope you're adorable."

"I'm not a kiddo Cash."

"Maybe not, but you have that innocence about you when you talk about the holidays."

"There's joy about them even when I'm walking through the darkness."

"You're a poet."

"What do mean?"

"You have a way with words that far exceeds my own."

Hope opened the book to an inscription.

She read it aloud. "To my heart, may you only know peace and love from this day forward, CB."

"Do you like it?"

She leaned against him and said, "I love it."

She kissed his cheek.

"The question is how close do you feel to me now?"

"I feel closer to you than I've ever felt to anyone."

"I feel the same about you."

Hope chuckled. "I thought I was dead. I got so lucky to catch the railing. And to have you to pull me up."

"You climbed up the building. You gave me a reason to live."

"You gave me my life back. You protected me and Nancy, there's so much to thank you for. Now you're mentoring me."

"I thought I would resent having you on the same album but instead I know it's going to be something special."

"Making music with you is like breathing air. It is magical."

"Magical indeed."

Nancy came zooming into the room and up onto Cash's lap. Hope smiled and laughed and said, "Aw, she approves of you."

"So it seems."

Hope set the earl grey aside and the book as well.

"I've always dreamed of a life like this."

"You mean of the rich and famous."

Hope laughed again. "No, one where I am at peace and am protected and loved and where I can create at will."

Cash cradled her cheek, "Well I am happy to make that happy for you."

"I'm just sorry we had to go through Bruce and a plane crash to get to this place."

Cash touched his forehead to hers and said, "But the point is we got here."

"We did, didn't we."

"Indeed we did."

And in the silence they kissed one another in a tender kiss. For the moment life was good.

Chapter 19

Mark was preparing the studio for Cash and Hope's arrival.

Things were difficult. Every night he went to bed thinking about the band. Thinking about a nosediving plane. Most important thinking about, Rose.

He knew his boss was feeling conflicted.

Cash wouldn't admit. He was on a high of new love and he wasn't facing the grief yet. He was too wrapped up in the shiny new toy named Hope.

It wasn't that Hope was a bad person, in fact she was an amazing one and a helluva an artist. She spoke to Cash in a way that others, especially women couldn't.

But grief was grief and needed to be processed.

Hope and Cash would be there soon.

Mark took a seat and listened to Hope's semi finished track for "My Journey."

He'd been thinking about Rose but when Hope's voice enveloped him it was her journey that came into sharp relief.

It was easy to lose himself to her vocals.

Tears came to her eyes and he thought of the night he fell in love with Rose. The moment she fell in love with him.

It didn't seem fair that Cash could move on so easily with a new woman and he was stuck in mourning.

But if Mark knew Cash, and he did know his friend, if he was not over it the mourning would erupt at some point and Hope might run screaming and not come back.

BRUCE LAY IN HIS CELL tapping the bed frame above him.
Repeating his arrest in his mind.
Knowing Hope was behind it.
Knowing Cash was behind her.
He was not through with them.
Truthfully he knew it might take time, but for as long as Hope had his he was not about to let her go.
As much as he loved her, he hated her now. And if he couldn't have her, he'd make damn sure no one would.

CASH WATCHED OVER HOPE as she slept.
The sun was coming into the room and it lit up her face just so.
She looked like as an angel.
She was an angel.
Fire and ice. That's what they were, and no one could stop them.
Not even that brute Bruce.
Hope had a way of making everything okay for him.
But Cash worried he would disappoint her.
She opened her eyes.
She smiled and said, "Hmm. I love the way you look at me."
"And how's that?"
"Like I'm the only thing that matters but you give me the space to be who I am."
"I love the way you look at me."
"And how's that?" Hope asked.
"Like I'm your my hero."
She laughed sweetly. "You are my hero."
"You're my hero."
"Well," she said, "over the years I've had to be my own hero."

"I totally get it."
"I feel like you do, especially more than most."
"How are your therapy sessions going?" Cash asked.
"They're difficult but worth it. Yours?"
"I've been a bit of an asshole."
"Maybe apologize."
"That path has been recommended more than once."
Both of them laughed.
"I have an appointment today," Hope said.
"I do to. But we have to go to Capitol."
"Do we?" Hope asked.
Cash looked at her quizzically.
"I feel like Mark doesn't like me."
"It's not that."
"Then what is it?"
"He's mourning and he thinks I'm dealing with it wrong."
"There's no right or wrong way to do it."
"Maybe, but know it's not you."
"That's good to know."
Cash kissed her.
"Time to roll."

Chapter 20

Cash sat in his therapist's office for the first time deciding to be completely vulnerable. In the past he had done it for a variety of reasons. But never for the right reason. To get better for himself.

He'd been court ordered before.

He done it for girlfriends before.

And he'd done it because the record label told him too as well.

But this was different.

He was in love with Hope. He wanted to love her the way she deserved to be and that meant being here to fix himself for his own sake.

Hope was unlike the others.

She saw him, really saw him. She saw through him. There was no faking with her, no hiding from her or himself.

The therapist walked in finally.

He had his journal, his pen and a cup of tea.

"Can I get you anything?"

"Healing tools."

"Are you really ready to work?"

"More than ever. I want to get better."

"That's good to hear."

Howard set his things down and settled into the chair across from Cash.

"Why do you want to get better?"

"To feel better," Cash said. "To function better. To be a better man for me so I can be better for everyone else."

"Healthy and noble."

"I'm glad you approve."

"Are you? Or do I sense some sarcasm."

"Probably both."

"Truth is a refreshing change with you."

Cash rolled his eyes and sighed, "I never walk through these doors to lie. Not to you anyway. I realize in the past the work I've done has been less than thorough. I want to change that."

"Well, Cash, where do you want to begin this time."

Cash looked at Howard. He seemed composed. But then the tears came and he croaked out, "The night of the plane crash."

"I think that's a natural place for you to start."

Cash nodded and bit down on his knuckle.

"I feel guilty."

"You're entire band and your girlfriend passed on. It's only normal to have survivor's guilt."

"I met Hope that night."

"You feel guilty falling for her so fast?"

"That's the thing. No."

"Not at all?"

"The way we met. It was intense and it resulted in us saving one another's lives."

"Yes it was broadcast on national television."

"Not all of it."

"What do you mean?"

"That night, in the hotel room, we spent it in the shower, holding one another. It was incandescent. Unlike anything I'd ever experienced. I needed her as much as she needed me."

"It sounds beautiful if complicated."

"It was, if I'm honest it still is."

"You never experienced that with Rose?"

"No."

"Ever."

"Never."

"That's okay. Sometimes emotionally we're not ready for it."

"Why when everyone was dead was I ready for it with a stranger?"

"Grief sometimes shuts us down, other times it opens us up."

"Howard, I have fallen hard for Hope. I love creating with her. But I feel like I'm cheating on my bandmates who got me here."

"That's to be expected."

"That's all you got for me?"

"Are you allowing yourself to feel these things?"

"They're fucking blinding at times."

"Cash you're a good man. Things will get better."

"How so?"

"Grief you will learn to emerge from it, feel it from time to time, and not stay in it."

"Promise doc?"

"I promise, Cash."

Chapter 21

Hope stood in the recording booth belting the lyrics to "Love Me Crazy". After warming up she sang a pop sugar rendition of a come on to Cash.

She didn't just sing it, she SANG it.

Those in the control room were impressed. Smiling. Knowing they were watching magic happen.

"Cash where did you find this songbird."

"She literally fell out of the sky," Cash said. "And don't you dare laugh."

Mark said, "I wouldn't dare."

"Yeah, right."

"Just tell her to keep singing."

"Her voice is the best thing to come into my life in years."

When she finished, Cash walked into the recording booth and kissed her passionately. Hope embraced him.

"How was your session," she asked softly.

"Better than you'd think."

"I need to go to my session."

"We should go to our session."

"I need a solo appointment first."

"Mark tell Donna we're done for the day. Hope is headed to therapy."

"Sure thing, Cash."

Hope took his hand and they walked out and onto the sidewalk.

"When the world comes together for the music it's a beautiful thing," Hope said.

"Indeed it is. When you sing it sets the world on fire."

"You're full of shit."

Both of them laughed.

"Maybe," Cash said.

"Definitely."

Cash grabbed a hold of Hope's hand.

"Christmas has been coming. Do you think you'd like to invite everyone over for a traditional holiday celebration."

"You never struck me as a traditional guy."

"Sometimes it time to start new traditions."

"There hasn't been joy in Whoville in quite sometime."

"It's time to bring it back."

"That's the understatement of the year."

Cash pointed up ahead, "Let's have lunch there."

"Farm to Table? My budget won't allow for it."

Cash stopped them and smiled slyly.

"Let me take care of it."

"You spoil me."

"You deserve it."

"I always thought if I was going to survive it would be a miracle. And it hasn't been. It has been several."

Cash wrapped her up in his arms and said, "Several."

"A series of several minor and major miracles."

"You flatter me."

"It has been perfect and God knows the holidays can bring on the stress, but it's been a long time since there's been a since of anticipation for me when it comes to Christmas."

"Have you gone ice skating before?"

"As a kid. And I hated it because everyone else was so good at it. People shoved me and bullied me. And I was always falling down."

"Let's go eat then I have a surprise for you."

"A surprise? Nancy needs me."

Cash whispered in her ear, "Something tells me Nancy won't mind."

"She really needs me."

"Nancy is safe and warm. Sam is watching her and Dawn is there with him to double check."

"Dawn is in town!"

"Yes, but that's not the surprise."

"Okay, I give."

"You give?"

"Yes."

Cash whirled her around and laughed.

"What's the surprise?"

"Just wait and see. Just you wait and see."

Chapter 22

Hope sat in the window sill thinking, remembering and staring out the window. Life in the last few months had been so intense she just needed a chance to slowdown and breathe.

She held her guitar, strumming it lightly, humming wordlessly at first then started thinking of covering a song that was so romantic but encapsulated this situation in an odd but dangerous way.

"Do you remember, when we met...I wanna tell you, how much I love you..."

There, in the quiet of the guest room she thought of the irony of the movie and the song, "Sea of Love," let her know the reality of a dream was possible.

Nancy came strolling in meowing.

Hope set her guitar aside and picked her up.

"Oh sweetie pie, you've led an eventful life. Are you ready for it to settle down?"

Nancy licked her face.

Hope pet her and snuggled with her.

"I need to go to my therapy session."

She sat her furbaby down and gathered her sheet music.

She couldn't believe the release day of the record was coming up so soon.

But it was and there was still so much to do.

Not to mention Bruce's trial and the coming confrontation there.

"Come on Baby, let's go get cleaned up."

Hope grabbed her things and Nancy trotted after her to the main room's bathroom.

As she rounded the corner she get humming "Sea of Love", Nancy wound her way through Hope's legs.

"That's funny my baby girl."

She walked into the bathroom and began to strip down.

There was a shower radio and she popped it on. "All I Really Want" started to blare and she started to jam.

She turned on the walk in shower.

She made the water as hot as possible.

Stepping she felt her troubles start to melt away.

Chris Cornell belted out "Like a Stone," and so did Hope.

She soaped up and allowed her hair to get soaking wet.

It wasn't long before she heard footsteps. The door to the bathroom opened. Cash stood there wrapped in just a towel.

He smiled, "Can I join you?"

Hope chuckled, "What do you think?"

Cash removed his towel and shut the door. He stepped in behind her and she turned around to face.

She trembled in his arms as they came skin to skin.

"This feels so right," Hope admitted.

"I've wanted our times together be special."

"They have been."

"This time changes everything."

"Promise?"

"I mean it."

He kissed her tenderly. She responded passionately.

Cash felt his blood surge.

His adrenaline raced. He leaned her into the wall.

Kissing her neck.

His hands roaming all around her body.

She sighed he took her legs and wrapped them around his body.

As he entered her body their eyes met and they became one. Tears came to both their eyes.

"I'm yours, Hope always."

"And I am yours."

THEY LAY IN BED, IN one another's arms. Their fingers linked.

"Christmas is going to special," Cash said.

"It already is."

He kissed her on the temple.

"True but I have been waiting all my life for this."

"That sounds mysterious," Hope said.

"It's meant to sound that way."

Cash laughed. "I want you to be happier than you ever been in the past."

"Ditto."

"Making love generally speaking has been a physical act for me. But with you it becomes spiritual. More."

"I feel the same way."

Cash kissed her and proceeded to take command in way Hope was safe in surrendering to ecstasy to.

Chapter 23

It was beautiful, the snow was falling, the Christmas Song was playing, and the Christmas lights were twinkling.

As she rounded the corner she watched as Cash put the finishing touches on the tree.

Nancy was curled up beside him.

He turned around and waved her over.

"This is beautiful, Cash."

"Your parents should be over soon. Dawn too."

He walked to the fireplace and picked up the lighter. Creating a fire.

Nancy sauntered under the tree.

Cash looked at Hope longingly.

"What do you want for Christmas?" Hope asked.

"All I want for Christmas is you."

Hope chuckled. "Ditto to you, kiddo."

"You family was very nice."

"They are. They can be very supportive when they know I'm happy."

Cash walked over to her and said, "As it should be."

He took her in his and started singing.

Hope swayed in his embrace.

Lana Del Rey played in the air.

"Dawn will be here too."

"Yes," he said nuzzling her ear,

The doorbell rang. But they kept dancing.

Sam appeared. "Sir, your guests have arrived."

THE GROUP SAT IN THE living room around the piano as Cash and Hope sat side by side. Cash tickled the ivories and Hope sang beautiful melodies.

"Have yourself a merry little Christmas."

It was warm and cozy.

Relaxed and intimate.

Cash started harmonizing.

There was a certain magic happening in the atmosphere.

"I'll be home for Christmas. You can count on me."

Sam came in with a tray of rich, gourmet hot chocolate in a pot along with matching mugs.

Cash stood up and poured and played host.

"Faye, your daughter is an angel."

"Other than making us worry for the last month I would agree with you."

"Cut her some slack. She was protecting herself and you guys."

Her dad John smiled, "And Nancy."

"And Nancy of course."

"Cash has made a profound difference in my life."

Cash put an arm around Hope and said, "And she in mind."

Nancy leapt up onto the piano bench alongside Hope.

"Awe sweetie baby," Hope cooed while petting her.

Cash gazed down at them.

It wasn't lost on Dawn.

It was a beautiful Norman Rockwellesque sight.

To often her friend had been in a dangerous situation with Bruce that none of them could do anything to extricate her from. Now she finally seemed truly and sincerely happen.

And for that they were all truly grateful.

LATER IN THE NIGHT Hope lay in Cash's arms thinking about what had transpired in over the holidays.

Being with her family and best friend again.

She and Nancy safe and warm and feeling the true meaning of the holidays.

"So are your dreams still happening?" Cash asked.

"Yes."

"That simply."

"Yes," she said, rolling over. "I've never wanted much but love, Nancy, and to sing. I've only ever had one of those things."

"Well now you have all of them."

They held onto one another and kissed sweetly.

"You're my hero," Cash said.

"And you're mine."

Nancy jumped up on the bed on them.

They giggled and laughed at the purity of her love and rejoiced in the joy of their love.

Chapter 24

Hope couldn't sleep.

Not with Bruce's trial starting the next morning and the stress of road testing the new album.

It was good to have her family and friends alongside Cash to help her through it.

She had a lot of decisions to make.

As she sat on the edge of their bed she felt the fast strums of a guitar melody building in her chest.

There was a song inside her that was dying to get out.

But when she thought about all that she had been through and all that she still had to do the guitar strumming got louder and louder inside her head. And her heartbeat thumped harder and harder.

She crawled out of bed and slipped into Cash's flannel shirt.

She grabbed her guitar and pick.

Quickly tuning the instrument she started singing softly.

"I don't feel right, but I break when you walk back through the door."

Hope didn't notice Cash.

She wasn't playing for Cash or even about him.

This song was filled with pain and regret, even rage, this song wasn't for Bruce but it was about their relationship.

Abuse was wrong.

There were people who would twist it to trap a woman or a man.

But no more.

She was free.

She looked up and Cash was there.

Tears flowed down her cheeks.

Cash embraced her and said, "I am here. Darling I love you. It's going to be okay."

"I don't want to go to the courthouse."

"I know you don't but there are things that have to be done for us to have peace of mind."

"Why do I have to do it?"

"You have more courage than I do. I know you don't want to see Bruce but by facing him down you're going to save countless lives."

"You promise."

"I do."

"And when we go out on the road it will be a magical thing."

"It already is."

Their foreheads touched.

"Maybe I should talk to my therapy."

"Afterwards for sure."

"Do you still think about Rose and the band?"

"All the time," Cash said. "Sometimes it paralyzes me."

"I feel so helpless."

"You're not."

"At times I feel alone Cash."

"Hope I can tell you, Nancy has always been by your side. And you by hers. She brought me to you when Bruce was on the loose."

"I was so afraid he would hurt her. I still am."

"I won't let him, no matter the cost."

"Bruce has a way of charming people, he charmed me. I feel so stupid."

"He love bombed you Hope. People falter in the face of that."

"Did I love bomb you, Cash?"

"No, we saved each other that night. And today I'm going to stand by you while the trial happens and we're going to face whatever happens together."

They kissed passionately and parted.
Cash knew they were fire.
In a relationship.
In an artistic relationship.
And as friends.
They were going to overcome whatever obstacles the world put in their path, Cash would see to it and he knew Hope would too.
"Make love to me Cash."
"Later, when the trial is over and there's no longer the need to fear today."
"Bruce will always be in my head."
Hope started to cry.
Cash took her in his arms and comforted her.
There was no reason to turn to more than kissing and embracing for the moment. They were due at the courthouse.
They were about to reclaim their lives.

Chapter 25

Hope and Cash walked into the packed courtroom and took a seat behind the assistant district attorney.

Taking Hope's coat Cash helped her sit down.

She wasn't the quiet, timid person begging for shelter.

No, here she was a pant suit dressed steely eyed warrior. She had waited for her day of justice and now that it was here she was there to accept it full on.

Judge and bailiff entered. The bailiff announced the judge's presence.

"All rise, for your honor Melissa Goodman."

"You may be seated."

The world had been waiting for this.

He had been waiting for this.

Hope had been waiting for this.

Bruce no doubt had waited for the moment he could confront Hope.

Cash worried for her. All the bodyguards and all the security in the world could shield her heart when she would come face to face with Bruce, the man who had repeatedly tried to murder her.

Her rosary was wrapped around her hand, gripped tightly as possible.

Her foot tapped necessarily.

Cash covered her knee.

She swallowed hard, her chest tight.

But having Cash there was new and slowly her grip on the rosary loosened and her foot stopped moving.

Cash leaned in and whispered, "You got this kiddo."

"I know. Finally I know."

She kissed Cash's cheek.

He took her hand and they braced themselves for the end of one chapter and the beginning of another to their lives together.

BRUCE STIRRED, THE guards shackled him from ankles to wrists.

"Grenwood, it's your turn at bat."

He said nothing.

He was mean.

He was sullen,

And a brute.

He made his entrance under heavy guard.

All eyes were on him.

Heavy, judgmental, sitting from their perch of self-righteousness.

And there in the center of the circus was that bitch Hope.

With her would be Lancelot.

Didn't she know she was Guinevere and he was King Arthur?

He saw the way she looked at that rockstar.

She used to look at him like that.

Bitch, she was his.

Or she was no one's.

He watched Cash wrap his arms around her and cradle her head to his shoulder.

He went back to that night in the hotel.

She had told him it was over.

That when they got home she was packing her things and leaving. But he wouldn't know when or how.

He remembered looking for Nancy, but not finding her, going to work one day and her being gone.

He remembered hitting her and putting her through the window.

He remembered feeling like a god.

Seeing her shielded from him like some sort of monster engendered rage and jealousy.

He would take the stand and make the jury see she was not royalty, but a common everyday slut.

The fact that everyone felt sorry for them beyond his comprehension, why couldn't see it from his perspective.

Hope leaned on Cash, but it was different.

It wasn't in fear.

She thought she was ready to do battle with him. She hadn't the first fucking clue.

"HE THINKS HE HAS US right where he wants us, you know."

"He doesn't have the first clue what you're made of."

"No, he doesn't."

Cash smiled at Hope and said, "I'm gonna love this."

"Me too Cash. Me too."

Chapter 26

Later that night Hope stood in the shower numb and crying. The water soaked her body and ran down her skin.

Sitting in the courtroom all day had been a draining process.

Knowing Bruce was just feet away. Him looking at her with those cold, menacing eyes. All the while flashes of those terrible nights—one where her back went through glass and she dangled high above the Nashville sky. And when he reappeared the savageness with which he'd beaten her was too much to accept.

Sitting in the courtroom she could no longer run.

Running from Bruce.

Running from fear.

Running. Just running.

Even if it was into Cash's arms she didn't want to run anymore.

The water was hot, so hot she could barely stand it. Life was that way.

She just wanted Bruce to disappear.

She just wanted to make music. Alone. With Nancy, and with Cash.

Life could be good if she could just figure the combination out.

Cash wanted to talk but she didn't have it in her on the way home.

She turned her face up into the running water and thought about what kind of life she could really have now and if Bruce was truly out of her life for good.

She hadn't talked early, but maybe, maybe over dinner and drinks.

THEY ATE QUIETLY AT the table.

Hope still couldn't bring herself to talk. Reliving the trauma that brought her to Nashville initially was too much.

Cash reached out and touched her hand. "Are you ready to talk about it?"

"Not really. The courtroom was where most of it was laid out."

"It brought that night back for me too."

"Intense."

"It was intense."

"I remember not thinking. And just reaching out and grabbing for the railing. And there you were, like some grief stricken angel. Ready to checkout himself."

"Truer words," he said softly.

"When do you think a normal life can begin."

"You're asking the wrong person."

She looked hurt.

He squeezed her hand.

"I only meant that I've been living in rockstar world for a long time. Now if you ask me when can our journey begin I'd say as soon as this trial is over."

She squeezed his hand back.

"That sounds wonderful."

They both leaned back in their seats and the staff began to serve them.

Like something out of a fairytale.

Cash smiled at her and said, "It's all going to be okay."

Hope couldn't help but feel the doubt creeping in.

All she had ever wanted was to sing, write, and play guitar.

And be free of Bruce.

Cash was an unexpected addition.

A beautiful surprise that brightened her life in ways she had never counted on.

He was a prince charming. A knight in shining armor.

Who showed up to defend her honor against the dark knight, Bruce's dark prince who had no redeeming qualities whatsoever.

She wanted the world to know they were a team.

That they were unstoppable.

That when they finally took the stage they would rule the world at the musical realm and perhaps no one could touch them.

Cash said, "We will bring him down."

"I keep telling myself that, but I think about how close to death I came and Nancy has escaped his wrath but for how long."

"You let me worry about that."

"You can't watch me forever."

"Maybe not, but between the two of us we can make it work."

"Maybe we stand a real shot at a new normal."

"I think so."

"I think so too."

Nancy leapt into her lap and Hope snuggled with her.

Cash beamed.

Hope was lovely.

Hope was kind.

So was Nancy.

And it struck him hard just how much he loved them both.

Chapter 27

Cash and Hope walked into a small dive, guitars slung across their backs. As they moved through the crowd murmurs rippled through it like a wave.

"This is crazy," Hope whispered in Cash's ear.

"This is about you."

"Cash this is about you."

"Trust me, this is about us."

"Scandals do that."

"Wait until they hear you sing."

Hope chuckled. Cash kissed her cheek. They plugged their acoustic guitars in and took a seat across from each other.

Hope began strumming her guitar.

The drum started and Cash sang the harmony and Hope was joining on the melody.

It didn't take long for the audience to start clapping and joining along.

As Cash sang in harmony Hope belted out the melody the crowd clapped along until they came to a stop.

The crowd was racous and happy.

Cash and Hope looked at one another in triumph.

"See I told you they would love you," Cash said.

"They loved us," Hope said with tears in her eyes.

Cash took her hand squeezed it.

The crowd ate it up.

Hope looked out over the crowd and a thrill went through her.

She tuned her guitar and she and Cash began playing together once more. They rocked the house.

And for the next few hours she was able to forget about the trial, forget about Bruce, and focus on the future.

THEY WALKED INTO THE house late in the night. Hope was jovial and jubilant. On a musical high she whirled around and kissed Cash passionately.

Cash kicked the door shut and locked it.

They kissed again.

"You are so lovely," he said.

"And you are so sexy."

"You were amazing."

"I have never been on such a high."

"Hope, there's nothing like performing."

"Babe, as long as you are by my side there's nothing I can't do."

"Are you ready to testify in court tomorrow?"

Hope ran her hands through his hair and said, "As ready as I'll ever be to testify."

"I'll be there. And remember Bruce won't be able to touch you."

"I really want to be able to believe that."

Cash held her tenderly and stroked her hair.

"Believe it baby."

She smiled and cocked her head to the side.

"I do."

Nancy rubbed against their ankles they looked down and chuckled.

"How'd I get so lucky?" he asked.

"I don't know," she said, "but as soon as I figure it out I'll let you know."

They kissed and slowly folded to the floor.

THEY WOKE TANGLED IN the bed sheets.

Cash watched her as the sunlight hit her face. She was peaceful and full of grace.

She smiled at him.

She whispered, "This feels right."

"It does," he admitted.

"There's no one else haunting me," Hope said.

"It's just you in my heart, beautiful."

"There are those who got me here but I want you. Love only you. I think we can have a future together."

Cash twirled her around and they started to hum their single which stood to top the charts.

"Cash I meant to tell you anything was possible."

"Hope the night I met you I realized that, you are amazing."

"So are you Cash. Your voice soothes the savage beast."

He clasped her hand in his and kissed her wrist.

"I've waited my whole life for you," he said.

"And me for you."

They kissed and when they made love the world fell away.

Chapter 28

Cash sat in the studio, alone with a cup of black coffee and a burning Marlboro red. The songs strangely sad.

After such a triumphant night he was mired in thoughts of the loss of his band and Rose.

Rose was there haunting him.

Mark was grieving but the album was coming together nicely.

He was grieving, but he genuinely loved Hope.

Her name imbued his life with everything he wanted. But the craving for a night at the bar and drinking the pain away was there just the same.

He took a drink of coffee and a drag off his cigarette.

Piano keys came from the guest room. Hope's delicate voice came floating into the studio. Breaking and cracking at just the right places.

Piercing his heart and finding the grief he was trying to hide from.

A tear slide down his cheek.

He stood up and wandered to the guest room watching and listening.

She played her keyboard. And gently sang her heart out. Her pain wrenching it's way out. Tears were flowing down her face as they were coming down his.

His own pain was being unleashed.

The loss of his friends and compadres was intense.

The guilt over Rose was just as bad.

Her heart gutted him.

As his gutted hers.

He slid to the ground next to her and they hugged.

"That was beautiful."

"Thank you, Cash."

They wept.

"Tell me where do you find lyrics and vocals like that."

"I find that usually pain speaks to truth. And that truth leads to healing. Bruce broke me in ways that simple words don't articulate and certainly can't fix."

Cash tucked her hair behind her ears. "I think you just fixed me."

She leaned against him.

"I can't believe I lived to tell the tale. It's because of you."

Cash stroked her hair.

"I can't believe I did either."

"Cash, what if Bruce gets out of jail."

"He won't."

"I didn't ask that."

"You are a rockstar. A warrior. A fighter."

"I know, but Bruce is a predator. Fighting him is unusual. And a constant battle."

"You will not face him alone."

"Promise."

"Forever. Now come on. We both have to testify today."

They stood and headed to the shower.

HOPE TOOK THE STAND. Her hand on the bible.

She took the oath.

She looked to the jury, then to Bruce who smirked, she braced herself.

She looked one last time to Cash, then finally to her attorney.

She took a deep breath.

The assistant DA led her strategically through that night, for the millionth.

"What is the moment you remember the most Ms. Wells?"

"Freefalling."

"Freefalling?"

"When he hit me I went through the window. And I fell. For a few moments I thought I was going to my death."

"And then what happened?"

"I caught the railing and Mr. Cash Grenwell pulled me to safety."

"And then."

"I was housed at Cash's home. And Bruce broke in."

"What did Bruce do?"

"He beat me and shot me multiple times."

"Are you sure?"

"Positive."

"That's all your honor."

Bruce leaned over and whispered. His attorney looked at him strangely.

"What."

"No questions."

"There's no other way to win."

"I said no questions."

"Why?"

"Just no questions."

His attorney sighed and said, "No questions your Honor."

Bruce and Hope locked gazes.

Something was up.

She just didn't know what was going on.

Chapter 29

Hope sat at the bar in the basement in Cash's man cave nursing a glass of wine. It had been a long day.

From the song that morning to testifying and wondering what Bruce was up to, she was drained.

She took a drink.

Bruce always was one step ahead.

She certainly hadn't thought he'd pull that.

No questions?

She sipped her wine.

Cash came downstairs with food from the Bristol Bar and Grille.

He presented the food and poured himself a shot of bourbon.

"I'm not hungry," Hope admitted.

"You gotta eat, love."

"I have no appetite."

"Why?"

"Bruce is planning something, I know it."

"You can't know that."

"Cash, I know Bruce, he has tried to kill me. Twice. I know what drives him and he wants me dead. Among other things."

"I'm sorry. When you're not used to being hunted it makes you blind to certain things."

"Like I'm a constant target."

"You are not a constant target. You have love. A wonderful furbaby. And you're getting ready to head out on tour to support an amazing album."

"I have been through a lot."

"You've earned your success."

"I haven't succeeded yet."

"On the contrary I think you have."

"I escaped and survived Bruce."

"You landed a record deal."

"I protected Nancy."

"You are a heroine. You saved my life."

"We saved each other's lives."

"I miss my family."

"You're about to be out on the road for an extended period of time, you can bring Nancy but extra two feet animals is problematic."

"So this is the star is born treatment."

"Your family would be happy for a show or two but road life in and of itself is a hard thing unless you are a musician yourself. And even then it can be isolating without bandmates or a romantic partner, and believe me my bandmates kept grounded even if the groupies and girlfriends couldn't."

"What makes you think I can ground you where the others couldn't."

"You see me. I mean really see me. You make me want to put down roots. But at the same time you get the performance side of me."

"So I see you. Do you see me?"

In a way, when Cash looked at her now there was an innocence and purity to her that made her vulnerable. Looking for approval.

She reached out, her hand trembling and touched his cheek.

It was magic.

In a world of hatred and ugliness she was all that was good and beautiful.

He thought back to the morning and her lyrics, who was I made/who do I love now/forgive me my faults and flaws/I love the blue eyed angel/and hate the dark eyed monster.

She was an angel sent from God above to save his soul.

All he wanted to do was take her in his arms and make love to her. Sweep away both their pain and make them feel everything good.

He wasn't close to his family but for a time he had been burdened by them.

He hated admitting that, but he used dream to escape the hell that his home life had been.

His father had been an unwell man, using drink and cigarettes to self treat mental illness. And at times he had followed the same path.

He prayed he never fell down that path again.

He prayed hard.

He didn't want to fall down that rabbit hole.

Cash pushed her food towards her.

Holding up a fork he said, "Please, Hope. Eat. The trial is almost over and Bruce will never be a problem to you again."

Hope turned to him, smiled sadly and said, "Okay baby, okay."

Chapter 30

They were leaving.

"I'm not getting on a plane," Cash said firmly. "A bus will do."

"Cash, you're being ridiculous," Sam said.

"Am I? Everyone else is dead. They were on that plane and I wasn't. I lost Rose. That was bad enough. Hope is on another level. If I lost her, or she lost me, I don't know what I'd do."

Hope walked up with Nancy and the rest of her things.

"Bus, right?" she asked with a smile.

Sam looked at Cash tightly. "I'll let Mark know about the change."

"You're the best Sam."

As they stood there Hope's heart raced. The tour bus pulled up, Tina Turner's "The Best" blasting for everyone to hear.

Hope turned to Cash and said, "They know how to send you off."

"Send us off beautiful."

Tears sprang to her eyes. "Del used to call everyone that."

"I call you Hope."

The doors to the bus opened and Mark appeared.

"Your chariot awaits."

"Thanks man."

"I know you need this. And so does Hope. You both have been through a lot and are about to go about proving yourselves in a way neither understands yet."

"All I know is we both have a long way to go personally. But Jesus, when she opens her mouth and sings it's a choir of angels."

"She definitely casts a spell when she does. Not only that she's a good influence on you. Now let's get on this bus."

Mark went to take Nancy, and Hope clung to her. "Take these instead.'"

She extended her suitcase to him.

Mark took it and said, "I got you. You and Nancy are safe."

"Hey, hands off."

"Chill boys. There's enough of me for everyone."

"You're funny."

"Thanks," she said. "Where's my room?"

"Straight to the back."

"But that's where Cash is sleeping."

"Is there a problem?" Cash asked.

"No, I just guess we're going public."

"That okay?"

Hope smiled quietly, "No, no problem."

Cash put his arm around her and kissed her cheek.

"Our relationship is not just about trauma. Or trauma recovery. It's about love and healing and getting to that place of joy together. Do you see it? Can you see it?"

"I see the light. It shines through your eyes."

"Angel it shines through yours as well."

Sam hopped on the bus.

"A crowd is forming, we need to be going."

"After you Angel," Cash said.

Hope went to the back and slid onto the bed. She cuddled with Nancy and said, "We're definitely not in Kansas anymore girl."

Chapter 31

Cash slept fitfully.

He stood in a field. The wreckage of the plane engulfed in flames. The incinerated bodies laying strewn across the field. Rose's body staring back at him.

He woke up screaming.

Hope sat up and cradled him.

Rocking him.

"It's okay."

"How," he whispered as he shook in her arms."

"I'm here."

He turned her face into his shoulder and was weeping uncontrollably.

"Tell me," Hope whispered.

"I can't."

"I told you all my secrets. I sat on the courtroom stand. I faced my demons. I continue to face them. If I can do it, so can you."

"I dreamt I was in a field. Standing before the wreckage of the plan. The smell of burnt flesh hitting me. And there was Rose charred and burnt empty sockets staring at me. I failed her. I failed me. I failed all of them. Now I'm afraid I'm going to fail you. That I'm going to fail us."

Tears slipped down his cheeks. Hope tenderly wiped them away.

"The only thing you did was choose not to get on that plane. There is nothing sinful about that or surviving it."

"What if more danger comes your way?"

"Then we'll face it together."

"What if it's not enough?"

"It is enough."

Hope kissed his tears away. "Success is coming our way. And we can dedicate the album to Rose and your band."

He took her wrist and tenderly kissed it.

"To new beginnings."

Hope smiled and said, "To new beginnings."

They kissed passionately.

Cash laid her to the bed and rolled on top of her. "I love you, beautiful."

Slowly they began to make love. Their eyes locked on to each other. He entered her and all at once it became clear. He'd been waiting for her for an eternity.

THEY STOOD ON THE STAGE for sound check.

It marked the official moment their tour started.

It was a club packed to see them sing their hit song, "Healing Me, Healing You."

As they walked out onto stage hand in hand.

Cash was finished looking. He had found his other half. His home. He got down on one knee.

The crowd roared.

"Will you Hope, be mine forever?"

Hope nodded yes.

The crowd roared again.

Cash picked her up and kissed her.

Mark smiled, tears in his eyes. He open his locked and looked at a picture of Rose. Then closed it. It was good that Cash had found the lock to his key. But he wasn't there yet. Not yet.

Made in the USA
Coppell, TX
21 February 2026

71844451R20059